The Maidens' Journey

EAMON GABRIEL

ISBN 979-8-89112-137-9 (Paperback)
ISBN 979-8-89112-139-3 (Hardcover)
ISBN 979-8-89112-138-6 (Digital)

Covenant Books
11661 Hwy 707
Murrells Inlet, SC 29576
www.covenantbooks.com

In this Home...

We work hard and make sacrifices. Music is usually playing and it speaks to the soul. Books are read and schedules overflow. Our children are loved, inspired, and supported to the fullest. This home is where our dreams are made and where our struggles become triumphs.

—Unknown

"Lo, children are a heritage of the Lord: and the fruit of the womb is his reward. As arrows are in the hand of a mighty man; so are children of the youth." (Psalm 127:3–4)

New Beginnings

The east wind blew through the willows, sending sheets of moss-laden gusts upon the shoreline. The day had finally come for their departure. The ship had been prepared as best it could. The great dragon's head on the front of the ship served as the entry into this new adventure they would soon undertake. Its fiery mouth was slightly open, bearing the wooden teeth and forked tongue leading to this new land they sought to the west. The men heaved load after load, onto the deck as the women prepared the children, bundling them in soft furs and sheepskin boots, seeking to protect them from the cold of the sea. Looking west from their known land, the men and the women both knew nothing of what was to come and feared for their children. The land they had here was scarce as it had filled with many families seeking their futures. The tide was out, and the boat's underbelly was in full view, resting on the earth slightly bowed to one side as the post for the sail was being pushed and pulled by the gusts draping the shore.

It was a fine ship, sturdy and well-built. While untested in open waters, the builder himself was among the families who would make this journey. Some ten families would join him and his kin and seek their fortunes to the west. Their new settlement would be one of equality under their new-found beliefs brought to them by a simple man. He would bless their journey to create this new land. He appeared to be a small man in build, at least as compared to others, but he possessed a keen inventive mind, and his faith was all but limitless. The other men in this world in which he lived were of a greater build and possessed physical strength that he could not compare with, but they knew they would be of need of him in this foreign and wild land in which they lived. He wore no fur or armor but only a robe of wool, and his heart sought not adventure as his fellows did but truth.

Thomas was his name, and he knew no other to be called this in this once foreign land on which he stood. He had become well-loved in their way in his time with these new friends. His travels had already brought him from his home in the Irish isle to their native land of Norway and then onward to Iceland, where they now stood, preparing to move even further to the west to a land very few had ever seen. His path had been laid before him, and he would follow it.

The bulk of this longship was soon filled to its capacity with all that they would take onward, and the time had come to prepare to board and depart. The tide shifted and set to moving in slowly, circling the ships and letting everyone know their time of departure was coming. With all of these grand things going on about them, no one noticed the two little girls, off to the side, two friends from as far back as they could remember, even though they were several years separated in age. They were now separating by distance, and they were to say goodbye.

The older of the two, Aurora, had to be strong for her younger friend. These two friends, having never been any more than a building apart in the entirety of their young lives, were now to be separated by the great sea. Austin, the younger, would be getting on the ship to build this new land in the west with her father, Tyr, the man who had chosen to lead this expedition west to the lands known as Greenland. Tyr was a large man having great strength and was a mighty warrior among his people. Austin loved her father, but she had never known her mother and was at times distant from him. Luckily, Aurora's mother had been around since the very beginning, as far back as she could remember, and loved her like a daughter. The two girls knew, as well as anyone, what the rise in the water had meant, having lived by the ocean all their lives. Their time was short, and they would soon need to say goodbye. Austin felt tears welling up in her eyes and hugged her friend. Aurora remained strong for her friend and hugged her firmly back, only releasing when Tyr called his daughter to board the ship.

Austin, being as young as she was, had a hard time letting go, but Aurora was a strong young girl and knew that they must part. Aurora's mother kept her distance from the two girls and watched as her child's friend was to board a ship for lands not well-known, and they may never see one another again. A tear began to appear in her eye as she watched, but she, too, was a strong woman and held it back for her daughter's sake. Austin walked aboard the ship and was followed by her father as the ship was pulled by the rising tide into the ocean, and the oars pushed off the earth beneath the water. Aurora's toughness soon faded, and she ran to her mother and was hugged. Her eyes no longer were able to control the tears that came forth as if a river dam had broken.

Aboard the ship, seated in the stern of the boat with her father, Austin, too, had broken down as she looked back toward the shoreline that was quickly disappearing. Tyr held his young daughter and told her, "We shall return, my girl."

She could hear his sincerity, and it made her less sad at that moment. The tears, which had been flowing like a waterfall now only trickled like a light mist on the sea air.

Aurora's mother had no such words. She merely hugged her girl and drew her close as if trying to draw her pain into herself with every teardrop staining her dress. She was a strong woman and knew that, sometimes, there were no words for some hurts, though, she wished there were. Her husband, Magnus, approached, and they turned and walked toward their home. He, too, was a large man, a head taller than Tyr, and possessed a powerful build from working the land. He was no less a warrior than Tyr and protected his family as all Viking men should. Magnus was the chieftain of this village and held his responsibilities as the most important of duties.

On the Home Front

Aurora's heart was breaking, and yet the day still went and came again. That night, she cried herself to sleep, missing her friend, and her mother could only comfort her, but that had been enough. The next day came early as it always had, and Aurora awoke feeling better. For a brief moment, she had completely forgotten that her friend had left, and she was happy. It took only a moment for her to come to the realization of what had happened the day prior, but as she was a strong, young girl, in spite of her nine short years, she bore up to the pain and resolved to move forward. She hoped that she would one day return to her. In the meantime, she had chores to do in preparation for the coming winter in three months' time. She dressed as she always had before and set about her morning chores before breakfast. As she passed the great cooking fire in their home, her mother acknowledged her with a smile, "Good morning, my darling child."

To which she replied, "Good morning, Mother, I will see to my chores. Do you need any herbs from the garden?"

"No, my girl, just see to your chores. Your father will be back from the shore soon."

With that, she walked out of the door and toward the garden as it was her chore to make sure there were no weeds taking over her mother's herbs. Plucking at the weeds brought her a sort of simple happiness, distracting her from her friend's being gone. She plucked and plucked at the weeds until they were all but gone as she saw her father approaching from the direction of the shore. It was at that moment she felt a small feeling of loss but quickly suppressed it as she saw the large fish her father was carrying as he approached. "Mother," she said as she ran toward the house to alert her that there would be fish for dinner that evening. Her father soon came along behind her and hung the fish from a large hook on the outside of the door. She had grown up eating fish like this, so it was a source of excitement, although it was a cod that they ate nearly every day. Her mother welcomed them both into the house and had breakfast for them on the table.

There, sat at the table, father, mother, her two brothers, and herself to break bread as a family. Father led them in their morning prayer, and they began to eat before returning to the day's chores. Aurora, having completed her chores for this time of the year, in an effort to keep her mind distracted, at first tried to help around the household with her mother. It was not long, though, that she found herself to be in the way and was sent away to find something to do elsewhere. There were other children around that were near to her in age, but she was not ready to be around other children yet. At only nine years of age, she was a very smart young girl, which often troubled some of her peers. She had a whimsical and inventive temperament, something she picked up from Thomas.

Thomas was a regular at their home for meals as was his way of sharing meals with the members of the community. He had no home of his own and resided out of doors, except in the winter, when he took up space in the communities' homes. He was a welcomed guest, and the children loved his stories and, of course, his silly Irish accent, which they playfully mocked him over all the time. He had a level temperament and took their jokes with a smile and often a witty comeback toward the adults in the room. Having been sent out of her house and not being ready to interact with the other children, she found herself heading toward the shore where she knew her father would be out either fishing or repairing the family's boat. It was too early to harvest and too late to sow, so he found himself dealing with matters that needed to be taken care of by winter's freeze.

Aurora made her way amongst the grass, in the direction of the mast of her father's boat. She could see it in the distance and knew she was close as it drew ever closer. After another moment of walking, she heard a rustling in the distance to her right and felt a brief moment of fear welling up inside of her. Her muscles tensed in her legs as she braced for some action, of which she did not yet know what that might mean. She was only a young girl, after all, and was unsure what could be the threat. She cautiously moved forward, slowly and deliberately, still feeling the slight pain of fear in her belly. She was a girl of quick wit and knew that the fear came from just not knowing what was there, more than anything else. Soon she thought she would be out of the grass and could at least see what it may have been that was rustling the tall grass. This eased her initial fear, but it was what came next that made that brief relief completely end, and a deeper fear struck her heart.

In the distance, to her right, but sounding as though it was coming closer, a deep growl of incoherent words. She knew right then and there what was in those grasses, and she began to run to the quickly closing mast. Her heartbeat was as it had not been in her young life as the adrenaline pumped into her muscles. It was at that moment she felt a pair of strong arms scoop her up and cast her up onto a pair of equally strong shoulders, and her speed quickly increased. She had made it clear of the grass and in the direction of the boat but, suddenly, looking back, she saw what had been behind. Her eyes now looked upon a troll that while not large, was no less dangerous in its appearance. The creature's stature was small, but its musculature was immense as was common, even with young trolls.

Out of what seemed like nowhere, her father came forward, holding a small hand axe and rushing toward the troll, crossing her path and hiding it from view. As soon as she saw her father step in to do battle with the troll, she felt herself shift again and found herself on the earth, safely and gently placed next to the boat. It had all happened so fast she could not even be sure what had happened and who had scooped her up from the grass, but she knew she was safe, and the feeling of fear quickly left her. It was not a minute later that her father returned. He had a splatter of blood across his shirt and scratches on his wrist gauntlets, but he seemed not to be harmed. He grabbed her up and hugged her deeply. No words need be shared between them. She was safe, and that was all that mattered to her father.

After what seemed like a long period of time, he placed her back down and strode over to speak with Thomas who was standing nearby. She could not hear their conversation but noted that they exchanged a strong handshake that she had only seen her father use with other warriors on the eve of a battle. Her father patted him on the shoulder and made his way back to his little girl to ask if she was okay. "Yes, Father, one of your men pulled me out of the grass," she said in a confused tone.

He nodded and told her to return to her mother on the path. She began to walk that way and was soon joined by Thomas who she scolded for not being around to fight the troll. Thomas laughed as they strode on toward her house. Thomas said, "Make sure you go tell your mother what has happened!"

Her mother was standing not a few feet away and had heard the exchange and gave Thomas a nod of appreciation for seeing her girl home. "Aurora, now tell me what has happened, quickly," she said as she ushered her inside the house and closed the door behind.

*****

The seas tossed the longship back and forth as the waves thrashed against the sides, causing the men to rein in the sails before they would drop them entirely to allow the ship to regain its composure. Austin sat where she was in the rear, when she had departed, tucked down among some of her family's things, bracing herself as Tyr had told her. Amongst the waters, a great back rose from the sea, drawing closer to their small ship.

Forward

The ship continued to be battered by the growing waves as the winds grew to a gale. The great back continued to rise from the deep, pushing the waves ever toward their ship as it moved in their direction. Tyr ordered the men of the ship to bring in the oars on the left side so that they would not be broken on the creature's massive spine as it brushed against the hull. The ship rocked back and forth as it pushed against the hull, again and again. Tyr reached for an axe that was tied to the deck of the ship and tore it free. Austin wanted to help, but Tyr told her to remain where she was and strap herself down so that she would not be thrown overboard. As he said this, another strike hit the side of the hull, knocking the axe from his hand, and nearly striking Austin before landing, lodged in the wood beside her. The rocking had dislodged some gear on board, and when it shifted, one of the young men was nearly tossed overboard, hanging over the side with his leg, caught in a loose rope that had been holding the gear down. He yelled for help as he struggled to get himself back aboard and free of the rope.

Tyr, having regained the axe, struck at the back of the creature, forcing it to move away as sheets of blood came from its now exposed spine. Three men moved toward the man hanging from the side and tried to drag him back on board. Tyr struck one final time, before the creature's great head came out of the sea, and its large teeth gnashed as it howled in pain before sinking back into the depths.

On the other side of the ship, the three men continued to try and get their fellow aboard. The rope was tight around his leg, and he was strung over the side, his face being bashed again and again by the waves, choking the life from him as he fought to right himself and get back aboard. The men were pulling him in toward the boat as quickly as they could when the creature's great mouth came forth from beneath the depths. Rows of gnashing teeth came toward their fellow. It was only by luck and sheer will that he was returned to the deck. He sighed a breath of relief when a large spike rose from the sea and speared him through his middle and jerked him into the sea rope still attached to his leg.

As the creature pulled him into the deep, the boat began to flounder on that side, and the mast soon started to lean and bow against the winds and the seawater that were splashing against it. The ship started to turn on that side, and it threatened to topple and send everyone aboard into the sea. Austin, in spite of the time she had spent on the water, was not yet the strongest of swimmers and feared the ocean, so she grabbed hold tightly of the ropes and her father's leg as he stood next to her on the deck. Tyr held the hand axe still and knew what needed to be done. Looking down at his child holding on to him for dear life, he reached down with his free hand and removed her hand from his leg and thrust himself across the ship. With a great push of his legs, he let the movement of the waves rock the ship, sending him to where he needed to go. Axe still in hand, he reached out with his free hand and sought to clasp the side of the boat as he flew off the deck. He found no grip and slid over the side and into the depths.

Austin had seen this and began to well up with tears in the belief that her father was lost to her as well as her mother. She began to dislodge herself from the ropes and move toward that side of the ship, when she felt the ship right itself, and the men pulled down the sail, allowing the boat to regain its footing in the waters. Making it to the side of the ship her father had gone over, she grasped the edge and began to peer over to see if she could find him. A woman nearby grabbed her and pulled her back from the edge and tried to keep her still. She struggled and managed to wriggle her way free from her and get back to the edge with her reaching to grab her back still. She managed to get a look over the side, and a magnificent smile came across her glowing face, making her golden, blond hair shine even more. There, on the side of the boat, with his axe stuck in the wood, hung her father. Austin screamed, "Father!" as she hung onto the side of the ship, being restrained by the woman.

Tyr looked up at her and, with a smile on his face, reached out to the hands that now reached toward him from the men who had heard her and came to aid him. As soon as he was clear of the side, he reached back and pulled the axe from the wood gingerly. As this tool had just saved his life, he treated it with reverence. Placing the axe on the deck, he bent down and hugged his little girl firmly and proudly because it was not only the axe that had saved him, and he well knew it. "I love you, my girl," he said with no hint of restraint, and he stood, still holding her in his arms. This moment was short-lived as the waves began to land on the deck, causing all aboard to hunker onto the deck by the rails to keep from falling overboard. Tyr regained his composure and cast his daughter, as softly as he could, back on the deck, toward a nearby group of women who caught her and held her tight, understanding that she was now their charge. Austin watched as her father took command of the men aboard, directing repairs to the mast, the oars being put back out, and the rowing beginning again. He took his place in the rear of the boat, manning the rudder as Austin was moved toward him, back where she had originally been when the trip started.

She lodged herself between the side of the ship and the supplies, which they had packed there, gripping the ropes and holding herself fast. Tyr looked down for a moment, ensuring she was secure, and returned to surveying the deck and the sea, continually shouting orders and encouragement to the men. These men were all skilled men of the sea, but this was not a journey any of them had made before. His eyes remained keen as he watched the bow of the ship move through the waves as they lashed against it, continuing to try and bring them beneath the depths as they moved onward. A young woman sat alone, toward the front of the ship, tears pouring from her face, mourning the man that had been lost, but no one could comfort her at the moment. There would be time for that later, once they had reached land. The sky bellowed and thundered with wind thrashing the air and trying desperately to sink their little ship. Tyr was cast from his post, a time or two, but returned swiftly to steer them through the danger. Men moved about, helping to row the boat as directed by Tyr as the skies began to clear ahead.

It seemed as though it had been an eternity, but the sun began to shine through the northern clouds again. As soon as the first glints of sun peered through, Tyr ordered the sail to be raised and the oars to be brought in. This was a welcomed rest for the weary men and the terrified but resourceful women. They began to pull themselves out of their burrows and set to gather up and check what they had lost to the waves. This duty fell to Austin as her father continued to steer the boat onward, cutting into the sea's receding waves. Men and women, alike, rested while they could. Some even fell to slumber, all the while Tyr stood at the rudder. He would soon be relieved and come to sit next to his daughter who had pulled some bread from their bundles stowed by his feet. "Eat, Father!" she said, knowing that he must be hungry after their troubles.

They sat together quietly, making a meal of the bread she had gathered. Neither knew how much longer their journey would go and sought the opportunity to rest. Austin merely sat next to the hulking body of her father, her small frame a speck of his, but she felt safe. She knew he had her and she had him to protect her until she grew big enough to protect herself.

It Begins Again

The ship moved across the waves steadily, to places no one aboard yet knew, but there was comfort in what lay in front of them after that storm the previous day and that creature that could have only been a monster from the deep. The waters outside their small ship were vast and seemingly endless, but at least they were calm, and Tyr was able to get away from the rudder and sit with his girl. "Our trip will soon be over. I am sure of it," Tyr said to Austin as her face showed her concern.

"We have been traveling for five days, Father. We need to reach land or begin to fish to gather more supplies," Austin told her father.

He replied, "I know, girl. I feel it on the next horizon. Do you trust me?"

Austin looked up at him, and her eyes glowing, she did not need to reply. The sun shone against her blond hair, and she did trust him. Austin rose to her feet to move around and stretch her legs, moving forward to the front of the boat where she found herself staring over the prow. The dragon's head rose in front of her, pointing to where they needed to go. She looked up at it, and while intended to be frightening, she found it brought her joy. There was a small carving near the eye, on the right side that she knew well. It was a small little smile that her father had put there for her when he had carved the dragon's head. She smiled as she turned and looked again over the prow of the ship. Only this time, her smile grew even larger as she saw the shimmering of a mountain in the distance, just over the horizon as her father had said. In her excited rush to return to her father, she could not help but trip over all the people and bundles stowed about the ship.

Tyr had returned to the rudder and already knew what she was excited about but allowed her to tell him anyways. "I see land, a mountain!" she said in barely understandable words.

Tyr looked down on her and said, "Point the way since you saw it first."

Excited, Austin turned and pointed toward the land, which was growing larger as it closed to their boat. Her finger, outstretched toward it as if drawing it into her, and soon they would touch shore. The moment was welcomed, and everyone was excited. They all wanted to get off the boat and see what there was to see in this wild place. Tyr took control of the crowd, arranging a few men to head off first to scout the immediate area to ensure it was safe for the rest of the people to take to the shore. The five men leaped over the side, onto shore, and made their way further inland, slowly and cautiously as Tyr had instructed. The people on the boat stood excited but also wary of what they would report when they returned. The children onboard especially began to become agitated, waiting.

The men soon returned and reported that there were no threats in the immediate area. That was good enough for now, but he ordered that a guard of the men without families be posted while they got the supplies on shore and the settlement started. Three men for two-hour shifts for the next few days. Austin began to untie the ropes that were securing the supplies they had packed aboard and set to carrying what she could off the ship. She was of a small frame, though strong for her size, was unable to carry larger items. Her father would need to take them for her to the shoreline. He had told her along the way that she could pick where they set up their camp. With this in mind, she wandered about within the perimeter the guards had set or, well, mostly where they had set finding a grove that she liked just outside. She was unsure what these trees were called, but she recognized them from their previous home as strong sturdy trees, and she felt that they would be a safe place to set up camp.

As if to stake claim, she removed the little knife Tyr had given her from its sheath and dug it into the earth at her feet. Turning immediately, she ran to find her father and showed him her spot she had claimed, hoping he would agree it was as good as she thought.

She ran about searching and soon found him by the edge of the waters, looking back in the direction they had come. Speaking to himself as he stood along the coast, "I will protect your child, and she will come back to you in time."

Austin heard these words but was too excited to show him what she had found to take any note of them at the time. Grabbing his hand, she tugged pointlessly at him until he regained his sense and followed her toward the trees where she had staked her claim. They approached until she could see the knife sticking from the earth where she had left it. They stood in the trees as she picked up her knife and cleaned it. She returned it to its sheath. She had been taught to never return a blade to its sheath caked in dirt, and she heeded her lesson well. Looking up at her father, she waited for his thoughts on the spot she had chosen. He nodded slowly after a long pause, and she knew that this was where they would set up their camp, and she would build this place to be a home for them both. She did not remember her mother, but she was told that she was a remarkable woman who built a comfortable home for her family. Austin sought to emulate this image, and although she was still a young child, she was well underway to being a fine woman under her friend, Aurora's, instruction. It was only then, for a moment, that she missed her friend.

Stopping her work, she sat for a bit on a rock, next to the trees, a place which she knew, from that moment, would be her place of thought, and felt her friend's being gone for the first time since their first day at sea. Austin looked round outside of her little grove of what her father said were birch trees and watched the work being done on all the campsites nearby. There would be time for this more at another time, but for now, she would have to be as her mother was and build this place. She set herself back to her work of preparing the ground for their tent, which her father would erect upon his return. He had gone to find meat for the camp and explore a bit farther into the surrounding area.

As darkness began to fall on their first day ashore, she could see her father and his band returning from the woods, carrying several animals they had hunted for the camp's meals. Her father was carrying the front pole of a large animal she knew to be called a reindeer.

Over his shoulder, he carried another smaller animal that he took to their camp for their dinner. Setting it down, he quickly set to arrange and build their tent before the sun went down. While he did this, Austin began to build a fire to prepare the hare her father had brought them. Stopping briefly to remove his flint and steel from his leather belt pouch, he knelt to show Austin how to spark a flame to the fire ring she had built. She knew this already but enjoyed that he taught her again and again. The fire took no time to light, and it grew to a warm blaze as this land was colder than where they had left from.

The tent was nearly built, and Tyr set to preparing the interior for their night's rest. The furs they had brought were laid on the earth to keep the chill off them, and the blankets of sheep's wool and further animal furs were set about to be used as blankets. Outside the tent, Austin sat beside the fire on a small log she had dragged from the nearby trees and watched the fire as it cooked the hare she had placed a spit over. Tyr watched for a moment to see if she would catch her mistake, but it was clear she did not. He smiled as he moved to lift the spit from the flames. "You still have much to learn, my girl," he said as he moved the hare a little higher, the flames did not touch it, but the heat cooked it.

"Sorry, Father," was all she could say.

He was not upset by this. He was happy she had more to learn from him. As the hare cooked further, he sat on the earth, next to her, on a piece of fur. Looking at her and clasping his hands together, she did the same, and they prayed for the food's swift completion, the animal's worthy life, and to the Father for their safe arrival to these shores. The hare on the spit had just finished cooking as they completed their prayer, and Austin was indeed ready to eat, her stomach had begun to make noises as she prayed with her father, and she snickered a little because of it. Tyr reached out to the spit and removed it from the fire and, using his knife, cut a few small pieces off the side and placed them in a wooden bowl that he had set by the fire, earlier that evening, and went to finish the tent while his daughter ate. Having just the final pole to set on the tent, he quickly came back and sat down again beside her and began to eat himself.

Not needing a bowl, he cut pieces from the hare as he ate, and a few more were cut for his girl. They ate well that night, after some days of bread aboard the ship.

Austin was happy, although she was still adjusting to this new place. Tyr watched her, making sure she was well-fed and as happy as she could be under the circumstances. They sat for a time, next to the fire, until Austin began to yawn, and he knew it was time to get her to bed. Standing and scooping in one fell swoop, he carried her over to the tent and cast her inside on the furs and wrapped her in the sheep's wool blanket to sleep. Turning to go sit by the fire for a short time longer while she settled into slumber, he looked up into the sky and took in the stars overhead. His mind was filled with the things that needed to be done to get this place built and turn it into what he dreamed it would one day become. He thought also of his little girl who lay asleep, only feet away. He quickly set those thoughts aside and stacked more wood on the fire and raised the sides of the tent, allowing the heat to reach them as they slept. He lay at the opening to the tent, taking another sheep's wool blanket, and shielding Austin in the back of the tent as she slept peacefully. The smile on her face was a promise for tomorrow.

Aurora

"The creatures grow in boldness as each day passes!" bellowed Magnus to his wife. Aurora stood only feet away and knew all too well of her father's troubles with the trolls in recent months. They seemed to come from nowhere and were constant trouble, but no one could figure out from where and why they had come. There had been trolls in the mountains to the north for years as she had been told but rarely did they venture this far south to the shoreline. She had always been told that trolls feared water because they could not swim. She did not know if this was true or not. It may have been something she was told to help her cope with trolls in general. Either way, she would head for water upon sight of a troll and hope she was told the truth. She still had not figured out how she had gotten away the last time and who had grabbed her, but she was grateful. Her father's tone had mellowed, and it was not anger that was getting him so excited. He was just frustrated with the issue at hand.

All the children, including Aurora, went outside into the herb garden her mother had built and searched for something to do. Aurora lazily picked at the weeds in the garden for a few moments before her father and mother stepped outside the door. Her mother had her arm wrapped around her husband's arm and her head on his shoulder. They briefly exchanged a glance before he began to walk away, toward the shed. Aurora was bored with her task already and thought perhaps her father could use her help, but before she made it there, he came back out with a quiver on his back, sword on his hip, and spear in his hand. She knew from past experience that this could not be good, but she still was interested, so she quietly and sneakily followed him toward the fields and then the woods. She was somewhat scared of the woods, but she was close enough to her father that she felt safe.

The woods were dark and scary, but she pressed on, her hand clutching the handle of the little knife on the belt she wore around the waist of her dress. She was close but not too close as he trudged onward, having been joined by some of the other men in the village. She was a smart girl and understood that they were going to deal with the trolls, once and for all, and to either kill them or scare them away from this area and back into the mountains. They move onward into the woods, confident and well armed. She followed behind, wanting to see the excitement of it all. She was cautious not to be seen by the men and trailed at a safe distance. They soon stopped ahead of her and began to fan out in a half circle, around something that she could not see in front of them. Aurora's father said something to the man on his left that she could not hear, and they all moved forward in unison, slowly striking the bottom of their spears on the ground as they moved with each step.

She moved a little closer, even more quietly and cautiously than before, until she could see what they were seeing. In front of her was a group of five trolls of moderate size, eating what looked like a reindeer. They squealed and squeaked as they ate and seemed to speak to one another with their tones. She drew closer still to see more of what was happening as the men moved in on the creatures who had not yet seen them. She found a stone that was large enough for her to hide behind and watched from there as the men yelled a war cry and attacked the trolls, rushing at them, spear pointed. As they bore down on them, the trolls yelled and ran about in every direction. Aurora found this amusing and giggled a little, but no sooner had she done that did three very large trolls come from the hills in front of the men and attack them angrily. They were very large and tore trees from the ground to swing like clubs that the men, including her father, were forced to fall back and create a better plan to fight them.

Aurora tucked herself deeper next to the rock to keep from being seen by the towering trolls as the smaller ones ran about, coming in her general direction. She was terrified and found that she had no voice as the five trolls ran at her. She was not sure if they had seen her, but she knew they were coming at her, and if they found her, she would be in trouble. She began to crawl away from the stone and toward a group of small birch shrubs. She felt something grab onto her leg, and her heart skipped a beat. She turned her head, and a troll had her by the leg and was pulling her toward himself. She kicked as hard as she could and finally was able to scream. She rolled over onto her back and, kicking both legs out at the creature, drew the knife from its sheath, and slashed out at the beast as it tried to get to her. Its hands tore at her legs and feet, scratching her deeply on her left leg, below the knee. She swung the knife quickly and ineffectively, trying to get the creature off of her. It was not a moment longer when she felt her shoulders being dragged in the other direction, and a spear came through the air, striking the troll in the head and killing it instantly.

She saw leather boots and coarse woolen trousers by her shoulder as she was dragged a short distance further and leaned against the rock she had originally crawled away from. She turned to see her father leaning over the rock, looking down on her with a face of both anger and thankfulness. He reached over, scooping her up, and drawing her into a powerful embrace. The men stood around covered in all manner of disgust, breathing heavily after their battle. Some were injured, and one lay on the ground, nearly in pieces. She was lifted to the heavens as high as Magnus could lift with his now one good arm. "Thank God you made it away from those creatures!" Magnus said with effort as he, too, was out of breath.

"Father, I was dragged away, and the creature killed," she said excitedly.

Her father had not heard her and placed her back down as his injuries had started to be felt. She stood a moment until she herself could feel the pain coming from her wound and fell to the ground, unable to hold her weight. A moment later, Thomas leaned over her and looked at her wound as he had done the other men. In his homeland, he had been a healer in the monastery and was well-versed in dealing with wounds. He bandaged her leg and began to rise before turning and handing the small knife back to her without a word. It was different somehow. It seemed a little larger and perhaps a little bit heavier, but her leg hurt so badly she did not give it much thought and tried to place it in the sheath but found it did not fit. She quickly slid it into her belt and was helped to her feet by Thomas and picked up into the good arm of Magnus as his other sat in a sling across his chest. Magnus was in a good deal of pain, and he was feeling it now, but so was Aurora. Her leg ached greatly.

They strode on back to the village, the injured men dragging themselves, and the body of their dead friend behind them to give a proper burial. Magnus was angry with is daughter, and he had every right to be, but for the moment, he let it pass. His arm hurt him far too much to deal with her at the moment. She sat clutched in his good arm tightly, and she knew that he was angry, and she would find herself in trouble at some later time but, for the moment, her pain was too much to deal with as well.

They returned to the house, and Magnus greeted his wife warmly. She, on the other hand, was not in such pain to lash out against her daughter for her foolishness. No sooner had Magnus placed her on the ground was her mother scolding her for putting herself in danger. Magnus was relieved but did not show that he would not have to scold on this occasion. Magnus went past them both and went to sit in his chair by the fire. The pain settling to an ache.

He knew he had been lucky this day. Looking over at his daughter by the door, he knew he had been very lucky, and he thanked God his daughter was so quick to get away when she did and believed she did have an angel watching over her. Magnus thought on this for a time, looking into the fire, before his wife and daughter walked past, heading to her bed to tend her leg. He knew he, too, would receive a lashing of her tongue in time, but for now, he just enjoyed this ache because he knew hers would be far worse.

Aurora removed what was left of her leggings beneath her dress, and her mother looked at the dressing and the wound that Thomas had tended. She was pleased by the work he had done and the state of the injury. It appeared it was already healing well. She had always marveled at his healers' skill, in spite of him being an Irishman. She stepped away to get clean water and fresh dressing and returned quickly to wash and dress the wound before telling her daughter to lay back and lift her leg on a mat, allowing it to heal. Aurora did as she was told and lay back quietly, her head still full of her mother's words, and her leg still in a great deal of pain until she drifted off to sleep. The pain in her leg ached, but she slept deeply and dreamed of her friend. She saw them running together through the fields, playing in her mind, and it brought happiness to her heart as she rested and healed. She was suddenly awoken by the sound of metal clashing against the wood floor and jumped to her feet. Her leg gave way, and she fell to the floor with a thud and a howl of pain. Her mother came in, yelling for her to get back into bed.

"Mother, what is going on? What was that loud noise?" she said through gritted teeth. Looking beyond her mother, she could see her father trying to put his chain mail over his bad arm to little success.

A Troubling Winter

Austin's hands felt the cold even through her soft sheep's wool gloves. She tried to be as helpful as she could repairing the doorframe that had collapsed in the gale of wind coming down from the mountains. It was soon clear that she was not of much help in this situation, and she moved away and inside to warm her hands next to the fire. She removed her gloves, and the cold burned her hands as they warmed next to the fire. Others moved about the hall that they had built together for the new village, stacking wood, preparing food, and some helping at the doorway. The weather had turned quickly on them, and they had not had time to fully establish the building before being forced inside it. The makeshift camps that sat outside were all but useless in this weather, so there were ten families huddled in this building intended as a feasting hall. They made do as best they could. Austin, having warmed her hands, stood for a moment, and looked around the space, taking in the state of the people residing inside. Her heart broke for them struggling as they were, but she, too, was in the midst of it.

Her father had gone out into the gale to hunt for food to sustain them while another few men to the boat to the sea to fish, something they knew well. She had absolute faith in her father to provide for her, and the men to provide for the village. It just seemed bleak, looking around now. The winds outside had gone on for some days and showed no signs of letting up anytime in the near future. Austin was nearly the youngest child present, but she was also the chieftain's child and sought to be of as much help to those around her as she could. She looked around once more, and it came to her how she could help. Walking around the space, she gathered all the children and brought them over to the firepit, and they began to tell stories.

She told stories she had learned from Thomas, although her accent was not as funny as his Irish accent, so some parts were not as funny as his telling.

Before long, some of the adults came closer and began to listen and were excited by her telling, in spite of having heard the tales many times before. It was in the middle of an exciting story that the men from the boat and her father returned to find her acting out a part and bringing the children to laughter. Tyr gathered the men from the boats, his men from the hunt, and all the others in the lodge and got the meat prepared for meals and to be preserved. The doorway had been secured, and Tyr acknowledged the good work among the men. The wind outside continued to howl and beat against the building, but for the time being, they were safe and warm.

Later, as each party found their beds Tyr sat with his daughter, next to the fire, and asked her to tell him a story. Austin smiled and told him one of Thomas' stories about the Shee of Ireland. She stood with the fire to her back, and he sat on the floor as was his custom and leaned against a bench, listening to her excitedly tell the tale. As it drew to a close, her fatigue had caught up with her, and she began to yawn. Finishing the story, she made her way to her bed. They had built themselves some pretty good beds of birch limbs rope and inland ferns they had collected to be used as mattress material. As she lay in her bedding, the furs snuggled around her as if they were still living, and she drifted into slumber. She slept soundly for a time until her mind began to race with the images of Aurora being grabbed by a troll and having to kick to free herself. She awoke with an abrupt scream that awoke Tyr. Austin looked at him for a moment and then laid back her head upon the matting she had prepared and fell immediately back to sleep. Tyr watched her for a few moments, and then he, too, returned to sleep.

Austin slept soundly from that point in spite of returning to the dream that had woken her, but it had changed. She no longer felt fear as she watched the scene unfold. She saw her friend being grabbed by the troll and her kicking and stabbing with her knife to get free. The part that had changed was that she now saw a robed figure reach down and grab her shoulders and pull her away from the troll. The figure threw a short spear at the head of the troll, killing it and dragging Aurora to safety, before disappearing into shadow as Magnus came into view and found her safe. When she woke the next morning, she felt as though this was no mere dream but thought nothing more of it. The children whom she had played with the night before wanted her to play games with them as the lodge rose and prepared to go about the day's chores and activities. Tyr watched as his child became the children's chieftain, and it made him proud. The winds outside had not let up, and it forced most of the people to remain inside.

Several days passed like this, and again, Tyr knew the meat would have to be hunted, but the last time was so hard he knew this may be harder still. The eyes of his people were beginning to look scant and wanting home. Austin felt this as well among the other children, and she mirrored it herself. They longed for their old friends and family that remained behind in Iceland. She thought of Aurora and the dreams she had been having, and they made her uncomfortable. Her mind felt cooped up in this building, so without anyone noticing, she ventured outside, bundled from head to toe in her fur and sheep's wool garments.

The wind was very cold and very strong. It nearly blew her over with each gust. As she walked no more than a few feet from the lodge, she smelled a foul odor in the air but could not see from where it came. It was not familiar to her, but it gave her a feeling of fear. As she shivered there in the cold winds, she stood completely still. She did not know what she should do, so she stood even more still than before, not even letting her shivers move her. Looking around in every direction, she tried to pinpoint the smell as it seemed to draw ever closer toward her. It was only then that in the snow white she could see what appeared to be a dark spot coming in her direction. A moment later, the shadow seemed to separate, and there were three shadows heading toward her. It was at this moment that she decided that staying still would not be the best idea, and she turned and ran as fast as her legs could take her back to the lodge. The odor seemed to dissipate as she entered the lodge, leaving the great entrance swinging as she entered.

Many were angered by this as the winds and the snow howled outside. A nearby woman scolded her, but she could not hear. She had been scanning the room for her father but had realized that he had departed to begin the day's hunt with four other men. Failing to find her father, she searched instead for Olaf, her father's second on this mission. She knew with Tyr gone he would be around to deal with the people. He was an older man but a good-natured man for a Viking. He was past his fighting years. Mostly he was content to deal with people's squabbles in the lodge. He sat near the back of the building, tending to a net. She ran up to him, the door having been closed behind her, and spoke at him in a frenzied tone. "Calm yourself, girl," the old man said as she tried to do as he asked.

She began to tell him of the odor and when she did, so his manner changed suddenly. "Did you see what it was that created the odor?" he asked manically.

Austin replied, "It looked like at first one shadow but soon became at least three. That was when I ran."

"You did well, girl," Olaf said with a hint of trouble in his voice. He rose quickly from there and let the net fall at his feet. Stepping over the crumpled net, he walked around, gathering men to the area of the building used for discussions and meetings. Austin followed him to see what was happening. The men all sat in the meeting area after he had gathered them, but they were still and quiet, not the boisterous talking that usually occurred. Olaf finally noticed her and, sternly but not with an angry tone, knelt down to speak to her quietly. "Have you told any other children of this?"

She listened but did not understand. She replied, "No."

He merely nodded and said, "Do not tell the other children. For now, pretend you saw nothing!"

His tone simply made her nod and walk away, trying to keep to her word as other children who had noticed the excitement and the meeting came toward her, asking questions about the gathering. Her silence spoke volumes, but she knew she would need to smile and suggest a game they might play. She walked away from that part of the building, and they found a ball they could throw about. This seemed to satisfy them all for a while. At one point in their play, the ball landed near the gathering, and she went to fetch it back. The quiet in the gathering was nothing she had heard before. She began to move away slowly, but as she drew away from them, she heard one word: *Draugar*!

The Creatures Stir

Austin threw the ball in the direction of a boy on her left, but it was without interest that she threw it. She did not know what the word the men had said meant, but she could tell that it was something that they did not like to speak of. The ball came around again and nearly hit her in the head as she thought about their words. She did catch it and pass it on as she had done before, but it was even more distracted than before. One of the little girls that was playing grabbed her by the arm and shook her for a moment, bringing her back to her senses. "I think we need to find another game," she said, pulling Austin to a pile of hay nearby and tossing her into it.

The children laughed as she stood with pieces of hay in her hair. Austin could not help but laugh as well as she threw the girl in the hay herself. It soon erupted into a battle for the hay. The laughter of the children rang through the building, livening up all that heard it. The men briefly stopped their conversation and looked toward the hay. Their faces did not change from their contorted troubled looks. A man standing at the door entered, followed by Tyr and the men he had taken. He soon joined the gathering, but the conversation ended quickly, and the men stood up and dispersed. Austin walked over to her father and greeted him warmly. She could see the concern on his face, but she knew not to ask at that moment. Her father, followed by one man, walked toward the entrance and stepped outside into the wind. He had not removed his outer layers, and she had noticed that he had picked up a spear by the front door. She decided to focus on the other children and their play and ask her father later what was going on. Perhaps he would be in a better mood later.

They stayed at play for some time before they all finally became bored of the game and dispersed. Austin saw this as a good time to speak to her father, but he could not be found. It was shortly after that she came to realize that he was still outside, standing watch. She put her fur on and went out the door to see him. When she opened the door, she saw that her father had his back to her, and he was talking with the other man on watch who stood with him. Their manner was tense. She walked up to her father who, upon noticing her, put on a show of happiness to see her that was not very good. "Father," she said with a mousy tone.

He looked at her and gave a faint smile, mostly, she thought, due to his being nearly frozen. "Go back inside. It is too cold out here for you," he said, trying to be as nice as possible but still stern.

She began to argue but thought better of it and returned inside. A few moments later, as she removed her fur and began to tidy their area of the lodge, her father approached and sat down on the ground next to her bed. "Sit, girl, while I get warm," he said, clearly very cold.

She did as she was told and began to ask him why they had guards posted outside the door. He shrugged but then thought better of that answer and told to her, under a code of silence to the others, that they believed what she had seen outside earlier was a creature known as a Draugar. He went on to explain that they were very dangerous shadow creatures that attacked villages. What he did not tell her was that, usually, the person who spotted them was in the most danger; he did not wish to scare her. This was why he decided to stay out on watch as long as he had. She could see he was tense and sat up next to him and placed her hands together, and he smiled and did the same. He led them in a prayer that had been taught to them by Thomas, and it made them both feel better. They sat together for a while longer, warming themselves in a blanket.

Austin was the first to rise, but she knew not why she did so. She simply began to walk, dressed as she was, toward the front door. Tyr noticed this as she grabbed the handle and began to open it. He jumped to his feet and hollered for someone near the door to grab the girl and drag her back inside. He ran over as fast as he could but was too late. From outside the door, an arm shrouded in pure darkness reached for her as she cleared the archway of the door, grabbing her by the arm, slowly pulling her outside the door further. People nearby saw this and grabbed at her while Tyr ran faster than he had ever run before and dove to grab her legs. He latched on to her legs like a tick and put all of his considerable size into weighing her down. Olaf was thrown a spear as he ran to help and thrust it at the dark arm, landing the point right above Austin's head, striking the creature. It let out a howl, but it was not a howl of pain but of anger as the hand was torn away from Austin's arm, and she was dragged into the building. The door was slammed behind them all, pulled shut by the force of the creature's anger.

Olaf yelled for the fire ring in the middle of the lodge to be loaded down with wood and be kept burning throughout the night. Tyr set a watch for the front door with orders not to go outside but to stand inside, making sure the door remained shut until the sun shone through. Austin was taken to her bed and tied to the beams to prevent her being drawn out again until morning. The fire blazed brightly as well as torches burned, keeping the building interior as bright as day while they all tried to sleep or stand the door or fire watch until morning. Tyr sat by Austin's side, shield on his left arm and axe in hand throughout the entire night, never taking his eyes off his little girl, mumbling to himself, "I promised I would protect your girl since she was taken from you."

Austin slept throughout the night, not having felt the draw of the Draugar. When the sun rose, Olaf and Tyr set men to tasks. Some were sent to cut down and gather as much wood as was possible. Others were instructed to gather food and water and fill the space not already in use at the lodge, floor to ceiling. While others still, including Tyr, were set to find the Draugar. The men were all told to return to the lodge two hours before the sun would set. The woman and a few of the older men watched the children and kept an eye on the lodge, keeping the keenest eye on Austin. Tyr had instructed them to never let her out of their sight. Austin, having not remembered anything of the night before, had no idea why any of this was happening. The weather outside had finally broken, and that was a good omen as they believed it. Austin was allowed to go out of doors but was always trailed by someone wherever she went.

The other children all had slept through the night's activity, some-how, and were acting as they did every day.

Several hours before dark, Tyr and his men returned, and he checked in on his daughter. Austin had been playing in the nearby field and was completely at ease with the day. She ran about playing with the other children in a new game they had invented. Suddenly, she stopped and sniffed the air, smelling a familiar odor that stung her nose. She turned and walked toward the darkness of the canopy of trees that were not yet cut by the men working still. Her guard followed and shouted to Tyr. Austin walked toward the trees in a trance, except for this time, she was fully aware of her actions but could not stop them. She placed one foot in front of the other. The small knife resting on her hip belt seemed to call to her, and she grasped it. Pulling it from the sheath, she slashed in front of her as a shadowed arm reached for her from the dark of the trees. The men with Tyr rushed into the trees, slashing and stabbing as they entered. Austin regained her feet and stopped and watched the arm being drawn back into the depths and heard the howls. This time, they were howls of pain as Tyr and the men stepped into the light once more.

A New Enemy

The sun rose, but no one could see it in the sky. Aurora stood in the doorway of their home, wrapped from head to toe in furs and sheep's wool. Nothing showed through, except her vibrant brown eyes. The weather was fierce, and it kept most of the day's labor from being done. Aurora was set on going outside. Her leg had been healing well, but she found that it made her stiff, and she wanted to exercise the muscles. She continued to have a slight limp, but Thomas said it would disappear as she healed and the strength regained. She stepped out into the snowy winds, which nearly sent her onto her butt with their force. She did not know where she was going but only needed to be somewhere else for a little time. The house was so small, after the time she had been stuck inside with her brothers who could not help but bother her. She loved her family but felt like something was missing, and she knew that she was missing Austin.

Looking around, blinded by the snow, she wondered how they were doing or even if they had made it there. She had to quickly put the idea out of her mind or she would dwell on it for too long. She walked over to the barn where she knew her father to be and entered, closing the door quickly behind herself. There was a fire burning in the pit that her father used for a forge, but he was not working with metal on this day. He, too, was working on the recovery of his shoulder and arm. He had built a device to both stretch and strengthen the weakened muscles from limited use. It had been some weeks since she awoke, finding her father gearing up for battle. She was thankful that on that day, at least the battle had not come. She knew that when spring came, it may still come. King Knut of Daneland was pressing on their world, and her father would not allow this to stand. While the winter took hold, he sent out messengers to the other chieftains in Iceland to seek a meeting. This was the day, in spite of the weather, that the meeting was to be held in the feasting hall at the center of the village.

Her father continued to train his muscles and prepare himself for the meeting. He knew she was there but was focused on his task, and she knew he needed to be. She watched the device as it worked and was interested in the creation. He, having seen her interest, spoke, saying, "Thomas showed me how to build this. He said it was from the Italians."

Thomas had proven to be well-traveled and experienced in many things over his time with them at their village. Aurora was pleased by this creation and watched further, before asking her father a question, "Why do you do that before the meeting today?"

Her father turned to her and called her closer. He leaned in and spoke both quietly and slowly, telling her an important lesson. He told her of the men that would come to meet and how he must show strength in times of his personal weakness. A man who would lead must be strong. She was worried that he may hurt himself in this exercise or in the display he must put forward and told him of her concern. Her father replied with a nod, "I understand, my girl. I will have Thomas nearby to attend to anything that may arise. He is a wise council in many matters."

Aurora liked the idea but had a question regarding Thomas. She asked her father, "How do you trust his word as mother says he is only an Irishman?"

Her father glared at her but said nothing at first. After a moment, his glare softened to a slight smile, and he said, "Your mother has her reasons for her belief, but do not think ill of both her and Thomas."

Aurora did not fully understand how she was to take these words. She did not know how she could think ill of her mother compared to an Irishman. She decided not to ask any more questions but to think about what her father had said and allow him to complete his exercise before the meeting. She stepped back and sat a little distance away, on a small stool, for him to finish. She would help him put on his mail and leather armor quietly so that no others would see. The mail was very heavy, and she struggled to help him but wanted to make the effort because she knew him to be a strong man in the best of times, and she also knew that an injury could be difficult. The time of the gathering was drawing near, and Aurora knew that she would not be allowed to watch them meet, but she was crafty and knew ways to sneak into the lodge. The other leaders or their messengers arrived one by one and were welcomed by Magnus and his wife to the feasting hall.

As they entered, Magnus' men-at-arms stood armed as guards at the great double doors. It took some time for all the guests to arrive, and the feasting had begun. It took several hours for the entire group to arrive. The great doors were finally closed to the delight of everyone inside. The weather had not grown better, and the fires of the great hall burned in an attempt to warm the building to limited success. Aurora had sneaked into the building as she had planned but needed to remain out of sight. She could not hear, so she needed to make her way to the head of the hall to hear her father speak. Moving her way in the nooks and crannies of the building, she made her way closer until she was almost where she wanted to be. It was at this point that she bumped into Thomas and feared she had been caught and would be scooted out of the door. Noticing her and understanding her desire to be involved, he smiled knowingly. His brown robes were large and seemed endless, so he scooted her behind him as he walked in a slightly strange manner due to her hiding. He moved toward the head table and took his place behind her mother, allowing the child to have a better view.

Aurora peered from behind his robes and took in the greatness of the gathering. There was much to see, but her father stood, and out of the corner of his eye, he could see his daughter and gave Thomas a sideways glance but turned to the crowd and began to speak. "My brothers, the Danes have pushed upon us. King Knut seeks to make a claim on our lands," he said with an intense tone. The room became quiet for a moment. Aurora somewhat understood the magnitude of what was happening as she had seen her father have dealings with the Danes before but never the king of the Danes. She was no longer sheepish and timid. She stood to her full height and moved away from the robes of Thomas and listened as her father continued to speak and the other men spoke in their turn.

The gathering was loud with periods of utter silence before her father returned to his chair and sat, thinking for a good while as other men continued to speak. She could see that his arm and shoulder were still hurting him greatly, and as he sat, he stretched and worked it, but soon, he stood once more, and the pain had all but vanished. Her father was a powerful man. Her mother had long since noticed her and likewise given Thomas a glare. He took the glare in his usual quiet confidence mixed with a small smile. She reached out and drew her daughter to her, giving her a half-scolding, half-proud look.

Her father had been speaking about discussing it further in the coming days, and each group of men set to their own discussions and planning. Magnus rose with his wife and told Thomas to take the girl, and they all moved away from the head table to a corner chamber, out of earshot. Her mother and father ushered her in and called for Thomas as well. The small door was closed behind them as they sat, and Aurora knew this could only mean a scolding. Thomas stood by the door, watching and listening to the goings on outside. The family spoke for a moment, giving her the scolding she had come to expect, but very quickly, Thomas was brought into it. "You understand the challenges we face better than anyone, and she should not be hearing such things," her mother said with a firm tone.

Thomas, with his head bowed, nodded and said, "She is a daughter of a chieftain, and while she has brothers, you know as well as I that she may one day lead this clan."

Aurora had never heard him speak in such a way to her mother, and her father simply sat there and allowed it. Aurora stood and somehow gained in height as she spoke, "You will not speak that way to my mother, Irishman."

At that, Magnus rose and towered over all others his very presence, causing Aurora to sit and bow her head. She did not see, but Thomas had not backed down at all at first but, after a moment, shrunk his size of his own decision. Magnus nodded with a subtle gesture and knelt before his daughter. He knew Thomas had been correct, and he spoke with her firmly but gently. "The Danes will be a great problem for us. Do you understand my meaning?"

She did not understand but pretended as though she did. They sat for a while longer, discussing the situation—Aurora sitting in the middle of her parents and Thomas standing watch at the door. Aurora did not see what good that would do. She loved Thomas but did not think of him much in the way of a man who could be of much use in a battle. He was not Norse and was a small man when standing amongst the other men. Magnus spoke directly to Thomas now. "What advice do you have in this matter?"

Aurora could not understand why he asked a monk such a question. Thomas immediately answered, "You should send official messengers to discuss peace, while at home, in secret, prepare unknown fortifications and seek aid from friends."

Magnus rose and walked with Thomas out of the room. Thomas followed behind, head slightly bowed. Aurora and her mother sat together, and her mother explained what troubles they had, knowing that her daughter only said she understood when asked by her father.

King Knut

Knut's kingdom lay far to the east of Iceland, but he was a greedy man and wanted it. He knew he did not have the strength of numbers to take the Swedes or the Norse to the north, but he sought the smaller groups to the west. Knut was still a youthful man who had many years left of kingship in him. His twelve-year-old son stood by his side, in the lodge of the Danes king and watched his father plan to take the lands of Magnus and his kin. Gunnar was a large boy like his father and wore a small sword at his waist. A gift given to him by his father, a short sword worn by the Celts of the Germanic lands. The map that was placed on the table before the king showed the known world, and it was west to Iceland that he wished to make his claim. An X marked the lands of Magnus, a symbol of his ownership.

*****

Aurora stood outside their home. The winds had stopped for a while, and she was able to move about more freely. Her leg had almost completely healed, and the limp was mostly gone. Thomas walked up to her door and, with a smile, asked about it. She replied that it had healed, and she was nearly back to normal. He was pleased with this and walked away without another word. She returned to watching the men, women, and even some of the older children working on various projects. Some were normal chores, but some of the projects she did not understand, and so she watched. Aurora's father had sent the messenger with all the pomp and circumstance they could muster to Knut, but in secret, he sent others to their friends and allies. The projects were to defend their homes, but they seemed strange to her. She began to walk among the various people working on their projects. Watching them and trying to figure out what it was they were making. She knew they were ideas from other lands.

The knife on her belt seemed to call to her, and she removed it from the new sheath. She did not know where it had come from. It had simply appeared one day and was a perfect fit for the knife. It was the first time she had looked at it and felt its weight. It was a completely different knife, more like a seax like her father carried. She found the weight a little challenging but knew she needed to adapt to it. It was good construction. In spite of her little knowledge of such things, she could see that clearly. She returned it to her belt and made her way toward one of the fortifications that the people were building in order to get a closer look at it. She did her best to stay out of the way. The whole village was busy with this idea that her father put together to defend them in case the Dane king brought a battle to them. Her father was somewhere in the village or perhaps out gathering meat. She decided she had better go back home because her leg had begun to pain her.

She walked slowly back, taking in everything that was happening, and it led her to worry about Austin for some reason. She knew that she was nowhere near this trouble but worried that she may have more trouble than even they did. She entered the house, expecting to find her mother, but she was nowhere to be found. Moving about the area of the homestead, she searched for her. It was not long before she found her in the barn where her father had been before the meeting. The forge glowed hot, and steam and smoke filled the room, venting out through the open door. Her mother stood over the forge, a piece of metal in the tongs in her hand. Her foot stoked the bellows, causing the coals to ignite and the metal to glow a bright orange. Aurora watched as her mother worked the metal. She had not seen her do this kind of work before. The sweat ran from her head and struck the coals with a sizzle.

Aroura wanted to go closer and see what it was she was making, but the heat kept her back. She could not figure it out, but the curiosity stirred her to watch further as her mother pulled the metal from the flames and placed it on the anvil, striking it again and again with her father's hammer. She could see that the efforts were exhausting.

Her mother placed the metal back into the fire and wiped the sweat from her head with the scarf she was using to hold her hair back, away from the coals. Her long blond hair needed to be restrained so that it would not get in her face or be lit by the coals. Aurora watched for a moment longer as her mother toiled and deciding not to interrupt. She turned and walked from the barn.

Magnus stood next to a table covered with papers. Thomas by his side, looking at the plans before them. The night prior, Thomas had drawn up, at the request of Magnus, these plans for the defense of their small village. They were simple enough on first look, and Magnus was not initially amazed by them. The first paper showed a drawing of a wooden wall wrapped around the main points of the village. A ditch would be dug right in front to keep attackers from getting too close to the walls. Magnus thought this was a great idea but was troubled by the amount of work involved and the likely little time they had. They bantered back and forth and concluded that the size of the wall should be restricted. Aurora walked over to the table and quietly listened to them speak. "It is decided," Magnus said, standing upright. "The wall will be placed around the lodge and the immediate buildings around it."

Thomas, seeing that Aurora was near, stepped back from the table slightly and nodded with a slight head bow. "The people not able to fight will remain in the lodge, and the outbuildings will be prepared with some surprises I have in mind," Thomas said with a light smile that Magnus understood to mean he had something interesting in mind.

"All the supplies will need to be placed here," Magnus said, pointing at the lodge's underground root cellar and rear corner of the building. "That will be your task."

Thomas nodded one more time and stepped back slowly to look to his task. Aurora came nearer to the table and looked at the plans or as much as she could see as the table was pretty tall. Magnus, seeing her walk up, scooped her up with this now to good arms and placed her sitting on the table's edge so she could see more clearly. He knew his daughter had an agile mind and would like to be a part of the planning in some way. Her brothers ran up from a group working in the building of the wall parts and stood, looking at the plans. Their father spoke to them, discussing the idea regarding the wall. Her brothers nodded, but Aurora spoke, "Why do we need a wall at all? Can we not just fight them?"

Her brother Harald snorted and turned to their father and said, "You see, father, girls know nothing of battle."

Her father gave him a deep look and said, "Perhaps she just has more faith than you do in our men's strength."

Harald was taken back by these words and felt a moment of shame. Erik stood beside his brother quietly, watching this all unfold, and clutching the short sword at his belt, stirred himself up to his full height, and tried to look larger than he was.

*****

King Knut sat in his council chamber, waiting on the messenger that had arrived from Magnus of Iceland. The man entered and drew closer to the king's seat before being stopped by his guards. "Speak your message," said the king with little interest.

The messenger relayed what he had been told to say by Magnus to the king of the Danes. As he spoke, Knut began to sit forward in his seat and, as soon as he was finished, stood and ordered this man be cast in irons and chained at his feet. Magnus had asked for peace, and this enraged the king because he was a king and the lands of Magnus were his. Magnus, a single chieftain of a small island away from the world. What could he do to deny a king? The messenger was returned, bloodied and chained, next to the king's chair. Knut looked down on him and said, "Listen closely, boy, to this plan and return it to your chieftain." Slapping the boy across the face with his hand, he returned to his chair and spoke to his counselor and his captains who had entered with the boy. Knut stood, clearing his throat, and spoke decisively, "Prepare three longships with a token party of some of the strongest men, and outfit them to raid on the lands of Magnus, but do not attack the chieftain's lodge."

He sneered as he spoke these words, leaving the messenger disgusted by this man. He knew that in spite of his decisions against his beliefs to take the message to the king of Danes that Magnus had been correct. Magnus was a true leader of men, and this king was a child upset because he could not get his way.

*****

Austin sat on the edge of her bed in the lodge, putting on her boots, and grabbing her sheep's wool jacket, she went out the main doors of the lodge, out into the sun. It was cold, but the sun shone warm against her face. Her mood was happy as she walked to the shoreline. There were several men there, including her father, building a smaller longship than the one they had arrived in. She was amused by this and walked up to inspect the work. Her father saw her coming and stopped what he was working on and greeted his daughter with a smile. Austin, seeing him smile, ran up and hugged her father. The other men kept to their work and prepared this ship to sail as soon as it was complete. "What are you making another ship for, Father?" Austin asked.

Her father took a moment before answering and said, "We have another journey ahead of us, my girl. One of great importance." Tyr said before returning to the task he had stopped when she came up.

Austin was excited by his words and thought that could only mean they were returning to see Aurora and their old home in Iceland. Her heart fluttered, and she was deeply happy. Her father looked at her as she scampered off to find some amusement or tell the children her new information. She ran to the field where some other children were at play and joined their game before she even knew what game it was, laughing her way through it. Her laughter was contagious, and soon the game came to a halt as the children just fell to the ground, erupting in laughter. The men by the boat who were just in earshot could hear the sound of happiness and were to be made happy, in spite of the chore they labored on and the reason why they labored. The boat would be ready in two days' time if they kept up the pace. Tyr, while also lightened by the laughter, scolded the men for delaying their work and set them back to their tasks with a reminder of the situation at hand. "My daughter is marked," he said as he labored to finish his part of the boat. He was relentless at his task, never ceasing until his hands could no longer work that day.

*****

The Danish longboats sat at the water's edge as the messenger was dragged to the lead ship and tied to the dragon's head. The king walked up and said to the messenger, "I hope you remember the message, boy. Tell your Magnus I am merciful."

With those last words, the longships cast off and rowed away from Dane lands, on their way to the lands of Magnus in Iceland.

*****

The small longship was finished, the stores for the journey were stowed aboard, and it was made ready to sail. Tyr spoke to Olaf as Austin stood nearby, watching the launching of the ship to begin the journey she had been waiting for several days. The oars were set, and the men that were to make the journey were aboard. All men without wives and children as few as could be managed for the trip. "Take care of these lands until our return." Austin and Tyr boarded the ship and cast off, heading east.

Together We Live

The younger children ran about, completely unaware of what may come in the very near future. The hills around their village were quiet and still. Barely a bird or beast could be heard. The wind moved steadily through the trees. Magnus hammered away on the fortification wall, laying in what would be the final assembly to be installed as soon as an attack was imminent. There was no door on the wall. Thomas had said that would be the weak point of the wall, and Magnus had decided there would be no weak point to this wall. It will stand through any attack. This he prayed as he worked. Having so little time to properly build and fortify, he could only hope and pray for the timber to be strong. The men toiled, digging the trenches that would surround the wall, and their sweat stank in the midday sun. Magnus stood among them, singing their praises and telling them the sweat they spilled today would keep their blood from spilling in days to come. The men cheered and set their back into their work with even deeper resolve. They were not all warriors as he was but simple farmers who, while brave, would fall before the armies of a king. Magnus would not allow this, and so he worked and planned, planned and worked to keep this from happening.

Thomas had removed his outer robes and, wearing only the inner ones, worked as hard as he could, exhibiting great strength, despite his smaller size. The walls stood, and Thomas set about preparing some other surprise for the attackers, should they come. Aurora's leg had fully healed, and her limp, while still there, was barely noticeable. She, of course, noticed and blamed Thomas for his having lied to her about it being gone entirely. She moved throughout the work, bringing water to the working men along with many other younger children. Her father would take none until the day's work was finished. She admired her father more each day as the projects continued. The work continued until sunset when all the men, women, and children retired to their homes to rest for the next day's labors.

Aurora was the first of her family to return to their home and again found her mother in the barn, laboring away at the forge. She watched again for a few moments and went into the house to get things ready for their evening meal, only to find it was all prepared and set on the table. Her mother really was a wonder. A minute later, her mother walked to the front door and splashed water over her head from the basin that stood by the door for washing. Seeing Aurora, she told her to clean up for the meal. Her father would be home soon and be very hungry from the day's work. They both went inside and finished the final touches of the evening's meal. It was not long until Aurora could hear her father's voice coming, and she went to the door to meet him. Her brothers were in the front of the troop, followed by her father, and Thomas talking with her father as they walked. They came to the door, her brothers running inside, knocking Aurora to the side.

Her mother had come to the door after their entry and greeted her husband. "Wife, we have a guest this night," Magnus said, both as a question and a statement.

Aurora, having regained her feet and stepped just outside the door, welcomed them both as her father entered, head held high, proud of the day's work. Thomas passed by the side of Aurora and her mother, head bowed, not making eye contact with her mother, his hood being removed as the courtesy of entering the home. Aurora was last to the table but first to try to dig into the food before being stopped by her mother. "We must give thanks, daughter," she said, looking in the direction of Thomas.

His eyes never looked up, but he began to speak the prayer of thanks for the meal that they would consume, the hands that prepared it, and the beasts that provided it. He finished by saying, "May the Lord bless and protect all of the children of this family!"

Aurora was finally allowed to grab the food and eat to her heart's content. All ate well, except Thomas who ate very little and drank no wine. All enjoyed the meal, and as soon as it was completely gone down to the last morsel, Aurora, her mother, and brother Erik set to clean up the table from the meal. Magnus takes Harald over to the fire and asks Thomas to come to have a seat for a while and discuss the next day's duties. "I must pray and prepare for the day's possibilities. Thank you for the meal. As always, it was very good," Thomas said, directing the last portion at Aurora's mother.

"Well, then, my friend, I will see you in the morning," Magnus replied while turning to speak to his son at the fire. Aurora watched as Thomas exited the house and headed in the direction of the woods, after putting his outer cloak over his monk's garb. She watched him as walked into the cold night and moved into the woods as he often did before times of trouble. In her head, she could not understand him but enjoyed his company still.

The evening proceeded as it usually did. Once the evening chores were completed, Magnus, or their mother, would often tell the children a story before they went to their beds to find their rest. Today was only different in that Magnus sat fairly quietly by the fire, stroking his red beard. He seemed in deep thought as their mother told a brief tale as all the children, as well as adults, were tired from the day's labors. Each took to their bed in turn and all, but Magnus was quickly asleep. Aurora's mother would be the last to bed after speaking with Magnus for a short time.

The next day came early. Magnus and his wife rose well before the sun and set themselves to the day's chores. By the time Aurora woke, breakfast was on the table, but her mother was nowhere to be found within the house. Aurora wondered aloud where their mother was, but her brothers only ate their meals and went to find their father to see what his needs were that day in the way of the defenses or stockpiling supplies in the lodge.

Aurora finished her meal and went to find her mother. No sooner had she walked out the door did she see that the barn door was open, and she thought that is where she would find her father at work in the forge. She went over and entered the barn to greet her father but found only her mother, again at work, hammer in hand. This time, she needed to see what she was doing and walked right up to her side to look. Her mother saw her there and told her to step back or she would be burned. Placing the hammer and tongs on the anvil, leaving the metal in the coals, she turned to her daughter. "I am sorry, Mother. I came to find you and found you here. What are you making?"

Her mother looked briefly over her shoulder, at the metal in the fire. "Why not watch but stand over there?" she said, pointing to a spot a safe distance from the forge. Grabbing the hammer in her right hand and the tongs in her left, she reached into the coals and pulled the metal out. Pointing with the metal to a wall in front of her, she said, "I am making you and your brothers' swords." On the wall where she pointed hung two swords almost completely finished. In her hand was the third. "This one is yours, my girl."

Aurora stepped one step closer to see the swords on the wall. She realized that they looked a little like the long knife she had in her sheath. Her mother began to hammer on the metal before placing it back in the coals to reheat. Looking over at her daughter, she saw the blade in her hand and called to her. "Let me see that blade, Aurora!" she said with a somewhat impatient tone.

She walked over and handed her mother the blade and took one step back. Her mother looked at it for a few moments, measuring the weight in her hands and admiring the craftsmanship. "This is a fine blade, Aurora. Can you handle the weight?" her mother asked as she handed it back to her, handle first.

As she took the blade back and returned it to the sheath, her mother asked one more question, "Did your father give you that?"

She replied, "Yes, Mother, but Thomas returned it to me after he treated my wound from the trolls."

Her mother said nothing more but turned and returned to her work, forging the blade for her daughter. It was just a little bit longer than the one she had and perhaps only a small bit heavier. Aurora looked at her mother and then at the wall where the finished swords hung, before walking out of the barn to find her father to see what help she could be.

Aurora's mother soon finished the blade and quenched it in the water barrel that stood alongside. Placing it on the anvil to cool further, she removed the leather apron from her neck and turned and walked out of the barn, toward the work to find Thomas. Failing to find him, she asked where he could be found. One of the women gathering supplies told he had gone to pray alone as he always did. Not knowing exactly where he had gone but having an idea, she walked from the village, in the direction of a small wood near the village.

She entered the woods and walked for only a short time before coming across Thomas standing in a grove of birch, his outer garment removed, bearing himself to the cold, wearing only his base layers. She could hear him praying as she drew near. Only feet away, she stopped and cleared her throat. Thomas did not turn until he finished the prayer. He turned his head down as always and waited for her to speak. "You gave Aurora that blade!" she said, half shouting. He did not answer but she already knew he had. After a moment, she said, "She is a child. That is far too large for her and too finely crafted. I know it is one of yours, Eamon."

Thomas slightly lifted his head to look her in the eye but did not finish the action. "My name is Thomas now," he said with his usual soft but terse tone. There was complete silence for a few moments before he spoke again while reaching the branch where he had hung his outer robe, "She needed a better defense from those trolls chasing her. Had I not—" He stopped speaking and continued to place his robes over his shoulders. She said nothing and neither did he before he walked past her, back toward the village and the work to be done. She waited a moment and returned to her home and the forge to finish the blades she had started. She was not angry. She realized she was annoyed that he was right.

The work in the village progressed as it had the previous day until the sun began to go down, and everyone returned to their homes again to seek rest. Aurora was the first of her family to reach the house, this time finding her mother standing in the doorway of their home. She ushered her daughter into the house and waited on Magnus and the boys to follow. Greeting them all as they came, they sat down to the evening's meal. As soon as it was over, she nodded to her husband, and he announced that they had something for each of them. As Magnus spoke, she got up from the table and grabbed the three wrapped blades and gave them each to the children. Removing the cloth, they marveled at the blades they each now held. Aurora looked at her mom, and they shared a knowing look. They all went to the fire, but instead of stories, they were told about the use of these and why they had received them from Magnus. It was a somber but necessary conversation.

Before everyone went to sleep that evening, they all shared an evening prayer and fell quickly to sleep, knowing the next day would come quickly as they had for some time. Even Magnus found rest quickly. His fears somehow lightened by the blades they all carried. The next day came early as had so many in recent days. Aurora woke shortly after her parents, her brothers still slept. Her mother making food for the morning meal for her family, her father already out of the house somewhere, planning or preparing. As she moved to the table, her father returned to the house, carrying three sheaths he had made for the new blades. Giving her mother the one for Aurora, she helped her attach it to the belt she wore before telling her she had better forgo the dress today and wear the trousers. Aurora changed into her trousers and returned to the table to eat. Her brother rose as well, and all ate their morning meal before going out with their father to work.

The morning was going well when a man on the beach from the top of a longship called the word that they had been dreading, *"Longships!"*

When word reached Magnus, he and Thomas stood up from the work to their full height and looked to the sea. "The time has come," he said loudly for all to hear. "Boys, get your mother and sister to the lodge now! And get your swords!" he said to his sons. Magnus moved to the shore to get a closer look. The boys ran in the other direction, expecting to find their mother and sister at the house. They arrived to find their mother putting on leather armor and wearing trousers. Aurora had gone to the shore at the call. She stood, watching as the ships drew nearer. Her father seeing her there, wearing trousers, a leather shirt, and her two blades, remarked, "You look just like your mother. God help me." He smiled but quickly told her to return to the lodge. She made no effort to move so he tried another way, bending down to meet her, he said, "Your mother will need your protection." Looking down, he saw the small blade and knew as her mother did where it had come from. "You have two fine blades. You are in good hands. Now go," he said, looking to the water.

She ran off but did not get too far before she turned and shouted to her father, "Father, I see another ship from the west." After watching the ship east go away from his village toward the north and south, he turned to see where this boat was headed. The flag bore Tyr's symbol, and he was in shock and terror as he said, "Austin!"

Vade Cum Deum